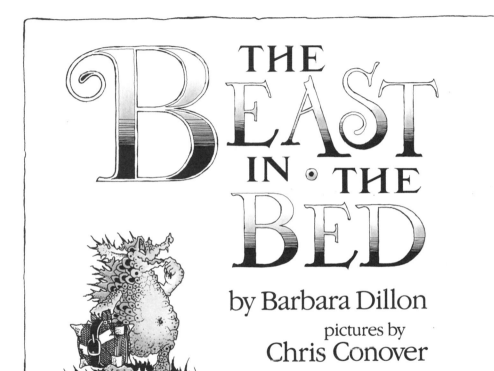

THE BEAST IN · THE BED

by Barbara Dillon

pictures by
Chris Conover

William Morrow and Company   New York 1981

Library of Congress Cataloging in Publication Data

Dillon, Barbara.
   The beast in the bed.
Summary: A small pea-green beast spends his days being a child's companion.
[1. Monsters—Fiction] I. Conover, Chris. II. Title.   PZ7.D57916Be   [E]   80-15069
ISBN 0-688-22254-4   ISBN 0-688-32254-9 (lib. bdg.)

To Lisa, Brook, and Nina.
B.D.

For Annie, who understands beasts.
C.C.

On a starry summer night a small beast, carrying a doll's suitcase, passed a cozy-looking white house with a big tree in
the front yard. Under the tree was a sandbox. Hung in the tree's
branches was a sturdy swing.

The beast crept up to the house and peered through the
living-room window. A little girl was sitting on the floor looking

at a picture book. The beast liked the blue pajamas she was
wearing and the way her hair hung on her shoulders in two
long braids.

Smiling to himself, he trotted to the porch and with his sharp,
little claws pried open the screen on the front door. Quick and
quiet as a mouse he scampered upstairs, running from room
to room till he came to the one with a dollhouse in it. He put his
suitcase down on the floor and took a big leap onto the bed.

Nice and soft, he thought to himself. I will like sleeping here
very much.

All at once he heard footsteps on the stairs.

It's her, thought the beast. And he dove under the covers,
giggling with excitement.

The footsteps skipped lightly down the hall and into the

room where he was hiding. Then they stopped, and he heard someone say in a surprised voice, "How did this funny little suitcase get here?"

The beast could not keep still a moment longer. "Surprise!" he cried with a laugh, popping out from under the covers. "Here I am!"

The little girl in the blue pajamas jumped in alarm when she saw the beast. She clutched her teddy bear tightly and called to her mother in a quavery voice, "Mom, there's a beast in my bed!"

"I'll come see it in the morning, Marcia," Mrs. Evans called back. "I'm reading now. Good night."

Marcia put out her hand and touched the beast's back. "I can't see you too well in the dark," she said nervously. "What color are you anyway?"

"A wonderful pea green," said the beast proudly. "With eyes to match."

"You are very little for a beast," said Marcia.

"Little is best," said the beast. "Then you can slip under things and in back of things and through things."

"Is that your suitcase?" she wanted to know.

The beast nodded.

"What's in it?" she asked.

"Nothing," said the beast. "It's just in case."

"In case what?"

"Never mind." The beast frowned. "I don't like to talk about it. Anyway, I'm tired. I would like to go to sleep now."

"Are you going to stay here all night?" Marcia asked.

"Oh, my goodness, yes!" The beast laughed gaily. "Tonight and tomorrow night and the night after that. I'll be around for a long time. But don't worry," he told Marcia, seeing the anxious look on her face. "You're going to love having me here. We'll have a wonderful time together, just the two of us." Then he wrapped his long, slender tail tightly about his body, dug his snout into Marcia's pillow, and two minutes later was snoring loudly.

And that was how the beast came to live with Marcia. Everywhere she went, he went too. Sometimes he was naughty. One day he poured hand lotion down the chimney of the dollhouse. Another time he scribbled with a purple crayon on the bathroom wall. But he was also a lot of fun. He built splendid castles in the sandbox and dribbled delicate turrets along the tops with wet sand. He could whistle beautifully and tell interesting stories. The ones Marcia liked best were about the different children he had lived with. She never tired of hearing what Mary Sue used to have for lunch; how Edmund had fallen from the seesaw and broken his arm; what Amy's mother had said when Amy cut off her little sister's pigtails with the nail scissors.

Sometimes, though, the beast grew sad thinking of all his old friends. "Once they went off to school," he would say with a sigh,

"nothing was ever the same again." And Marcia would have to take him down to her swing and push him high, high in the air to make him smile again.

Most afternoons Marcia and the beast went grocery shopping with Mrs. Evans.

"How come you never let grown-ups see you?" Marcia once asked, as the beast scampered along the aisles, darting behind the cart if Mrs. Evans looked his way.

"Because," he explained, "beasts make grown-ups nervous. Sometimes they even want to throw a beast out of the house."

"I would never let anyone throw you out," said Marcia fiercely.

   Slowly, so slowly that Marcia and the beast hardly noticed, the
sweet summer days drifted away. There were trips to the beach
where Marcia and the beast tumbled in the sand dunes and
splashed one another in the water. There was an afternoon at the
circus where they gorged themselves on peanuts and cotton
candy. There was a fireworks display on the Fourth of July that
sent the beast scurrying in terror under Marcia's bed. Marcia had
to hug him for a long while before he was calm enough to play
again. Marcia learned to do a cartwheel and grew a whole inch.
The beast learned to do a somersault and stayed the same size.
Summer could have gone on forever.
   But one morning, when Marcia and the beast awoke, there
was a chill in the air. Mrs. Evans announced at breakfast that it
was time to look for school shoes.

"School shoes?" cried the beast to Marcia. "Surely you're not going to school!"

"I'm going on Wednesday," Marcia told him. "I can hardly wait."

"Oh, no," the beast moaned.

"Don't worry," said Marcia, "we can still play together in the afternoon."

"It won't be the same," said the beast, shaking his head. "I know it won't."

The beast went along with Marcia and her mother to the shoe store, but he stayed in the car while they shopped. When they got home, he refused even to look at Marcia's new shoes.

"They're real leather," Marcia told him proudly.

"I hate leather," said the beast sulkily. "I like sneakers and sandals and, best of all, bare feet."

On Wednesday morning the beast, looking glum, watched Marcia get ready for school. "You're going to hate kindergarten," he told her while she was brushing her teeth. "I bet your teacher is going to be really mean," he said, as she tied her shoes. "I get to play outside all morning and you don't, so ha-ha-ha," he called

desperately as Marcia went skipping down the driveway to wait for the school bus.

Good, I will have the sandbox all to myself, he thought, as the bus rumbled into sight. And the swing too.

But it was no fun playing all alone, and he knew just what was going to happen next. Marcia would get busier and busier, and he would get lonelier and lonelier. It always ends up this way, he thought bitterly, with me getting dumped.

And so that very morning he made up his mind to leave the Evanses. Grimly he marched upstairs to Marcia's room, dragged his suitcase from the closet, and trotted down to the kitchen with it. From the refrigerator he got two slices of cheese, an apple, a cupcake, and some cold chicken. From the cupboard, he took four cookies, three pretzels, and two doughnuts. He crammed

everything into the suitcase, snapped the lock shut, and quickly
let himself out the kitchen door.

At the bottom of the driveway he turned around for one
last look at the house. "Good-bye, lovely swing. Good-bye, lovely
sandbox," he said. One green tear slipped down his nose as

he set off down the street. He just never could get used to saying good-bye.

It began to rain and continued all day long. When the beast's stomach told him it was time for supper, he huddled under a dripping oak tree and opened his suitcase. There wasn't much food left, for he had been nibbling it steadily. He ate the apple and a few crumbs of doughnut, and then he curled up in a ball with his tail tucked around him.

"Camping out is awful!" He shivered. "I'm glad I was never a boy scout." And he closed his eyes and tried to imagine himself safely back in Marcia's room, snoring peacefully at her side.

Next morning he woke up just as the sky was getting light. Raindrops falling through the branches of the oak pelted him like cold, little pebbles.

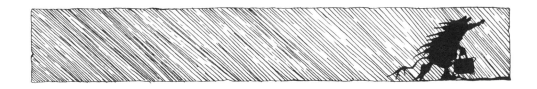

"Where will I ever find breakfast on a day like this?" he said
with a sigh. He stumbled to his feet, stretched once, yawned
twice, and trotted out to the road clutching his empty suitcase.

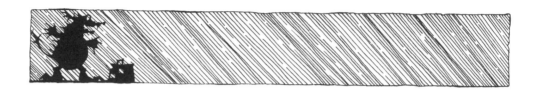

As he reached the curb a yellow school bus came rumbling around the corner. The bus stopped, and three children clambered aboard. Waving good-bye to them from the sidewalk was a small boy in a yellow slicker and boots. The beast's eyes glinted with excitement as the bus pulled away, leaving the boy in the slicker all alone.

Completely forgetting about breakfast, the beast shook the raindrops from his skin and sprinted nimbly to the boy's side.

"Hi," he said in his friendliest voice. "Want someone to walk you home?"

The boy jumped in surprise. He stared wide-eyed at the beast. "Who are you?" he asked.

"Beast," said the beast. "Who are you?"

"Ken," said Ken. "What are you made of, Beast?"

"Secret ingredients mostly," the beast told him. "Want to feel?"

As Ken leaned down the beast gave a quick little leap into the boy's arms.

"I'm very tired. Would you please carry me?" he asked.

"I think I better go home now," said Ken nervously. He tried to put the beast on the ground. "My mom is making waffles for me."

"Take me with you," begged the beast, clinging to Ken's sleeve. "I won't be any trouble. We'll have a lot of fun. I know all kinds of games and tricks. I know how to do a somersault. I'll teach you how to do one too."

Ken looked down into the beast's pleading green eyes. "I don't know if Mom will let me keep you," he said.

"She'll never even know I'm around," said the beast. "Honest."

Ken thought for a moment or two. "Well, okay," he said at last. "I guess it will be all right." With a grunt he hoisted the beast to his shoulder and set off for home, splashing through every puddle he came to.

"Did you say you were having waffles for breakfast?" the beast asked, snuggling against his new friend.

"Yes," said Ken. "With lots and lots of syrup."

The beast gave a happy sigh. Living with Ken was going to work out just fine–he could tell. And thinking of warm, sticky syrup and cozy kitchens, he closed his eyes and began to purr like a contented kitten.

ABOUT THE AUTHOR

Barbara Dillon was born in Montclair, New Jersey, and received a B.A. degree in English from Brown University. She worked for seven years as an editorial assistant for *The New Yorker* magazine and for five years taught prereading skills to three- and four-year-old children at day-care centers in Stamford, Connecticut.

Mother of three girls, Mrs. Dillon lives with her husband in Darien, Connecticut.

ABOUT THE ILLUSTRATOR

Chris Conover was born in New York City and studied at the High School of Music and Art and at the State University of New York at Buffalo. Since 1974, she has illustrated a number of well-received children's books, including *Six Little Ducks,* which she wrote as well. Currently Ms. Conover lives in Brooklyn, New York.